John Leech

Pictures of life and character

from the collection of Mr. Punch

John Leech

Pictures of life and character
from the collection of Mr. Punch

ISBN/EAN: 9783741190490

Manufactured in Europe, USA, Canada, Australia, Japa

Cover: Foto ©Andreas Hilbeck / pixelio.de

Manufactured and distributed by brebook publishing software
(www.brebook.com)

John Leech

Pictures of life and character

Prefatory Note.

*J*OHN LEECH, *whose humorous pictures of English life and character for so many years were the soul of "Punch" and the delight of nearly the entire English-speaking world, was born in London about* 1817, *and died there on October* 29, 1864, *at the comparatively early age of forty-seven. His drawings appeared in "Punch" soon after its establishment, and continued up to the time of his death. The social features and extravagances of England never found a more apt or kindly delineator, and in sporting scenes he was pre-eminent. One characteristic of Leech's drawings, as it is of those of his distinguished successor, Du Maurier, is* *their fidelity to English life. The slight exaggerations which the artist permits himself never affects the value of his drawings as accurate pictures of social conditions. "Many people," remarks Mr. Henry James, in his recent essay on Du Maurier, "have gathered their knowledge of English life almost entirely from 'Punch,' and it would be difficult to imagine a more abundant and, on the whole, a more accurate informant. The accumulated volumes of this periodical contain evidence on a multitude of points of which there is no mention in the serious works—not even in the novels—of the day. The smallest details of social habit are depicted there, and the oddities of a race of people in whom oddity is strangely compatible with the dominion of convention." It is to be further remarked of social caricatures in "Punch," that they are very rarely coarse, cruel, or bitter. There are very few lapses*

of taste; and for the most part they are remark-
able for their genial and even friendly spirit.
"*Punch*" has satirized every class, every social
foible, every form of national caprice, but it has
made no enemies, and to-day there are few held
in greater affection and esteem in England than
two of the most persistent satirizers of its people
—John Leech and George du Maurier.

The selections for this little volume have been
made with the purpose of representing the artist
in all the various forms of his work—as a hu-
morist, as a satirist, and as a delineator of character and social life. "*Leech*," says Mr. James,
"never made a mistake; he did well whatever he
did. He was always amusing, always full of
sense and point, always intensely English."

Contents.

Contents.

10 *Contents.*

Pictures of
Life and Character.

Pitiable Objects.

MR. DONE (*to Mr. Dreary*). "No! A don't know how it is—but I ain't the thing somehow! No embawassments or anything o' that sort. Can't make it out. S'pose its *overwork!*"

"Well, they may call this a health-giving pursuit, if they like; but give me roach-fishing in a punt."

MASTER G. O'RILLA. "Deaw! How shocking! There's another good fellah done for!"

COUSINS. "Why, what has happened, Gus?"

GUS. "Happened! Why, Charley Bagshot *gone married!*"

Startling Fact !

OXFORD SWELL. " Do you make many of these monkey-jackets, now ?"

SNIP. " Oh dear yes, sir ; there are more monkeys in Oxford this term than ever, sir."

Never carry your Gloves in your Hat.

Mr. POFFINGTON flatters himself he is creating a sensation.—(*Perhaps he is.*)

What must be the next Fashion in Bonnets.

Badly Hit during the recent Engagement with the Guards.

MAMMA. "Yes, doctor. She will sit for hours without speaking a word. She persists in wearing the same dress, and won't part with the bouquet!"

DOCTOR. "H'm—well, let's see; we must first get *the ball out of her head*, and then perhaps the nervous system may right itself!"

What they Said to Themselves.

HONORABLE MR. FIDDLE. " I wish that conceited ass, Faddle, would go!"

CAPTAIN FADDLE. " That stupid idiot, Fiddle, never knows when he's in the way!"

RICH WIDOW. " I shall be uncommonly glad when both of these simpletons take their departure."

Suburban Felicity. Gratifying Domestic (poultry) Incident.

Buttons. "Oh! Please 'm! He quick 'm! Here's the Coaching China a-clucking like hanythink. He've been and laid a hegg!!!"

Mr. BRIGGS tries (for many hours) a likely place for a perch ; but upon this occasion the wind is not in a favorable quarter.

Fly-Fishing.—Mr. HACKLE arrives at his favorite spot, where he knows there is a good trout.

23

Blind with Rage.

HUNTSMAN (*riding furiously over a fence to a Scarecrow*). " . . . You great fool; what the deuce do you stand pointing there for? Why don't you holler out which way the fox be gone? Blowed if I don't cut you into bits!"

Sporting Intelligence.—(From our own Correspondent.)

"The country is awfully deep, but the falling is delightfully soft and safe."

Helping Him On.

CRUEL FAIR ONE (*to silent Partner*). "Pray! have you *no* conversation?"

A Delicate Creature.

YOUTHFUL SWELL. "Now, Charley—you're just in time for breakfast—have a cup of coffee?"

LANGUID SWELL (*probably in a Government office*). "Thanks! No! I assure yah—my de-ar fellah! If I was to take a cup of coffee in the morning, it would keep me awake all day!"

Not a Bad Idea for Warm Weather.

FREDERICK. "Now, girls, pull away—don't be idle!"

28

First Languid Party. "Don't you find sea air very strengthening, Jack?"
Second Ditto Ditto. "Ah, vewy! I could throw stones in the water all day!"

Police Constable (*to Boy*). " Now, then, off with that hoop ! or I'll precious soon help you ! "

Lady (*who imagines the observation is addressed to her*). "What a monster !"

[Lifts up the Crinoline and hurries off.

Angling in the Serpentine—Saturday, P. M.

PISCATOR No. 1. "Had ever a bite, Jim?"
PISCATOR No. 2. "Not yet. I only come here last Wednesday!"

31

Not a Bad Judge.

ALIMENTIVE BOY. "My eye, Tommy, wouldn't I like to board in that 'ouse, just!"

Sound Advice.

MASTER TOM. "Have a weed, Gran'pa?"

GRAN'PA. "A what! sir?"

MASTER TOM. "A weed—a cigar, you know."

GRAN'PA. "Certainly not, sir. I never smoked in my life."

MASTER TOM. "Ah! then I wouldn't advise you to begin."

The Course of True, etc., Never Did, etc.

Here's poor young Wiggles anxious to meet the being he adores, but can not do so, because the newly-pitched boat upon which he has been sitting, has caught him alive O!

After Supper.—Strange Admission !

Mr. S.   "May I have the pleasure of waltzing with you, Miss Jones ?"
Miss J.   "I would with pleasure, *but unfortunately I'm quite full !*"

The Gentle Craft.

CONTEMPLATIVE MAN (*in punt*). "I don't so much care about the sport, it's the delicious repose I enjoy so."

Something in That!

"Now, TOM," said young JOE WAGLEY, "one of us ought to go on this side of the hedge, and one on the other; so I'll take this, if you will get over the stile."

"Oh, yes," replied TOM; "but how about the bull?"

Mʀ. B. goes out. His chief difficulty is that every time he throws his line, the hooks (of which there are five) will stick behind in his jacket and tr-us-rs.

Fly-Fishing.　A Nice Ripple on the Water.—" *Now for a big one !* "

Enter Mr. Bottles, the Butler.

MASTER FRED. "There! that's capital! stand still, BOTTLES, and I'll show you how the Chinese do the knife-trick at the play."

[BOTTLES *is much interested.*

A Fine Disposition.

AFFECTIONATE HUSBAND. "COME, POLLY, if I *am* a little irritable, it's over in a minute!!"

Scene—A Man's Rooms in the Temple.

(Steady man smokes a short pipe, and jaws at the young swell loung-ing in easy-chair.)

STEADY MAN. "A man must *work* nowadays, or he gets left behind. The only position worth having is what you make for yourself," etc., etc.

YOUTHFUL SWELL. "Oh, yes, I quite agwee with you about work. I don't mind work, you know, in a genewal way—but I object to what I call 'work of superwewogation!'"

STEADY MAN. "And pray what do you understand by that?"

YOUTHFUL SWELL. "Why—I mean I don't care to do anything I can get done for me!"

The Battle of the Pianos.

Alarming Occurrence.

CHORUS OF UNPROTECTED FEMALES. "Conductor! stop! Conductor! Omnibus-man! Here's a gentleman had an accident and broke a jar of leeches, and they're all over the omnibus!"

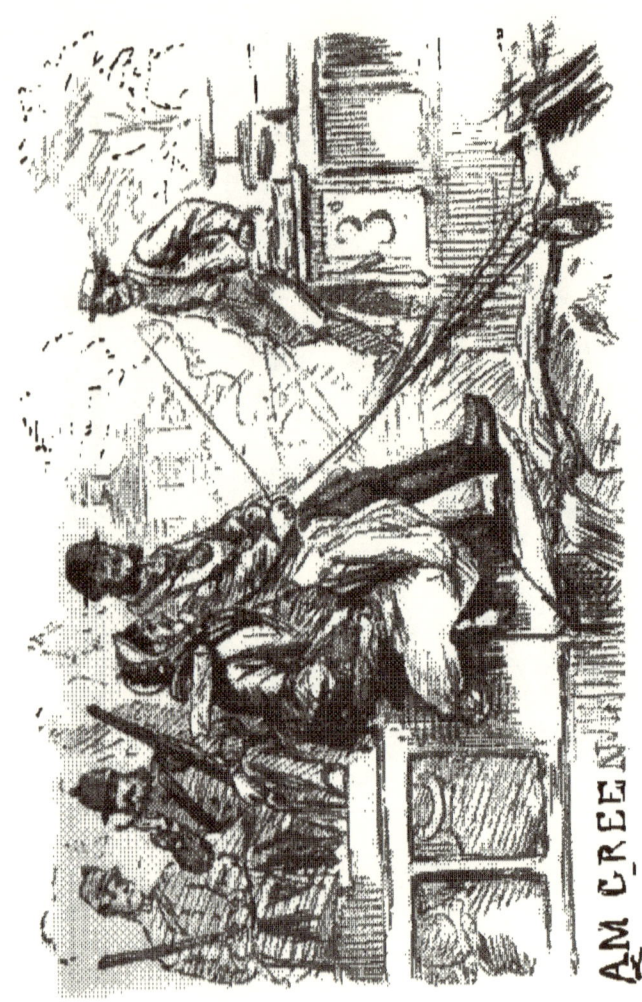

AM GREEN.

A Tit-Bit.

Omnibus-Driver (*in the distance*). "Holloa, Joe, now you've got your duck, I'll send you the peas!"

A False Position.

INDIVIDUAL (*who is not over-strong in his head, or firm on his legs*). "D-d-d-d-id waltzing—ever—make—you—giddy ? Because, I—shall—be—happy—to—sit—down—whenever—you're—tired !"

GIRL (*who is in high dancing condition*). "Oh, dear, no—I could waltz all night !"

46

Bloomerism !

STRONG-MINDED FEMALE. "Now, do, pray, Alfred, put down
that foolish novel, and do something rational. Go and play something on the piano; you never practice, now you're married."

First Elegant Creature. "A—don't you dance, Charles?"
Second Ditto Ditto. "A—no—not at pwesent! I always let the girls look, and long for me first!"

Private Theatricals.

Dismay of Mr. James Jessamy on being told that he will spoil the whole thing if he doesn't shave off his whiskers.

Poor Cousin Charles.

JUVENILE. "Why do they call those things Cousin CHARLES smokes cigarettes; eh, Polly?" . POLLY. "Well, dear; because they are little cigars, I suppose!"

JUVENILE. "Oh, then, would Cousin CHARLES be called a Captainette, because he's a little Captain?"

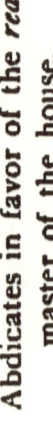

Abdicates in favor of the *real* master of the house.

Mr. Peewit has a little addition to his family—he is obliged to get his meals anyhow—and—

51

Poor Cousin Charles.

JUVENILE. "Why do they call those things Cousin CHARLES smokes cigarettes; eh, Polly?" . POLLY. "Well, dear; because they are little cigars, I suppose!" JUVENILE. "Oh, then, would Cousin CHARLES be called a Captainette, because he's a little Captain?"

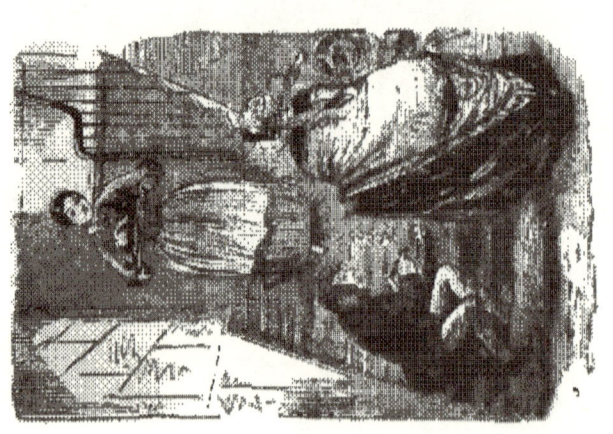

Mr. PEEWIT has a little addition to his family—he is obliged to get his meals anyhow—and—

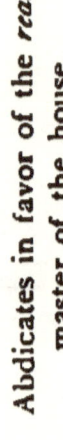

Abdicates in favor of the *real* master of the house.

A Cautious Bird.

LORKINS. "Well, I don't know about marryin'—for yer see, after the knot was tied, some other gal might be fallin' in love with one—and that would be so doooced awkward!"

STREET BOY (*in playful allusion to basket-carriage*). "Oh, look here, BILL! If 'ere ain't a swell driving hisself home from the wash!"

ARTHUR. "Mamma! isn't Mr. BLANQUE a wicked man?"

MAMMA. "Wicked, my dear! No! What makes you ask such a question?"

ARTHUR. "Why, because, mamma dear, when he comes into church, he doesn't *smell his hat* as other people do!"

54

Snow-Flakes.

STREET BOY (*to his natural enemy, the Policeman*). "Snow-balls, sir! No, sir! I haven't seen no one throw no snowballs, sir!"

DISCIPLE OF OLD ISAAC. "This wouldn't be a bad place if the fish would only bite, and if it wasn't for this confounded wasps' nest."

Well over, anyhow !

Elegant material for trousers;—only takes two men
to show the pattern.

The Marriage Question.

BROWN. "So, you're going to marry old Mrs. YELLOWBOYCE. Well, I think you're a dooced lucky fellah!"

JONES. "By Jove, I don't think the luck is all on my side! If she finds money, hang it, I find blood and — haw — beauty!"

Recollection of a jolly old paterfamilias we saw the other day, with some air-balloons for the chicks.

Consols at 90.

HUSBAND. "Well! I declare I'm quite glad it's a wet day. It will be an excuse to stop at home with my darling little pipsey popsy. What do you say, Dickey! eh? Pretty Dick! Pretty Dick!"

Consols at 80.

HUSBAND. "Go out for a walk! Nonsense! I've something else to do. I think, too, you might pull down that blind, unless you want the sun to spoil all the furniture: and, dear, dear, do for goodness' sake, JEMIMA, take that d—— canary out of the room!"

JONES (*who is naturally proud of his first-born*). "A little darling, ain't he?"

BACHELOR FRIEND. "H'm, ha! I see — young gorilla! Is he real or stuffed?"

A Bon-bon from a Juvenile Party.

FIRST JUVENILE. "That's a pretty girl talking to young AL-
GERNON BINKS!"

SECOND JUVENILE. "H'm — tol-lol! You should have seen her
some seasons ago."

BOWKER, who is fond of nice things for breakfast, and sometimes markets for himself, becomes an object of interest from having laid in a few bloaters, and half a pound of fresh Cambridge sausages, from Bond Street — and which sausages and bloaters are in his coat-pocket.

Flunkeiana.—Enter Thomas, who gives warning.

GENTLEMAN. "Oh, certainly! you can go, of course; but, as you have been with me for nine years, I should like to know the reason."

THOMAS. "Why, sir, it's my *feelins*. You used always to read prayers, sir, yourself—and since Miss WILKINS has been here, she's bin a-reading of 'em. Now, I can't *demean* myself by saying 'amen' to a guv'ness."

N. B.

These young gentlemen are not indulging in the filthy habit of smoking.—They are only chewing toothpicks, the comforting and elegant practice now so much in vogue.

[*Vide Public Streets, particularly St. James's Street, Regent Street, Bond Street, and Her Majesty's Park of Hyde.*

Dreadful for Young Oxford.

LADY. "Are you at Eton?"

YOUNG OXFORD. "Aw, no!—I'm at Oxford!"

LADY. "Oxford! Rather a nice place, is it not?"

YOUNG OXFORD. "Hum!—haw! Pretty well, but then I can't get on without female society!"

LADY. "Dear! dear! Pity you don't go to a girls' school, then!"

Master Jackey, having seen a "professor" of posturing, has a private performance of his own in the nursery.

Fearful practical joke, played with a child's balloon upon a swell.

Going to Cover.

Voice in the distance. "Now, then, Smith—come along!"
Smith. "Oh, it's all very well to say, come along! when he won't move a step; and
I'm afraid he's going to lie down."

The Shuttlecock Nuisance.

LITTLE GIRL "Oh, I beg your pardon, sir!—It was the wind as done it!"

Man on the Gray (*who comes Express pace over the Stile, and cannons against two quiet riders*). "Beg pardon, gentlemen, but my horse has got no mouth!"

Rather awkward for Tomkins

Young Diana. "I think, sir, if you would be so good as to go first, and break the top rail, my pony would get over."

73

Hunting Memorandum—Appearance of things in general to a gentleman who has just turned a complete somersault ! !

* etc., etc., represent sparks of divers beautiful colors.

Fly-Fishing.

PISCATOR. "Now, then! I think I shall get a *rise* here!"

Did you Ever?

OLD GENTLEMAN (*politely*). "Oh, Conductor! I shall feel greatly obliged to you if you would proceed, for I have an appointment in the Strand, and I am afraid I shall be too late."

CONDUCTOR (*slamming the door*). "Go on, Jim! Here's an old cove a cussin' and a swearin' like anythink!!!"

The Test of Gallantry.

CONDUCTOR. "Will any gent be so good as for to take this young lady in his lap?"

Our friend BRIGGS contemplates a day's fishing.

The Picnic.

CONTENTED MAN (*log.*). "What a nice, damp place we have secured; and how very fortunate we are in the weather; it would have been so provoking for us all to have brought our umbrellas and then to have had a fine day!! Glass of wine, BRIGGS, eh ?"

Friendly, but very Unpleasant.

LIVELY PARTY (*charging elderly gentleman with his umbrella*).
" Hullo, JONES ! "   [*Disgust of elderly party, whose name is* SMITH.

A Great Mental Effort.

FIRST COCK SPARROW. "What a miwackulous tie, FWANK! How the doose do you manage it?"

SECOND COCK SPARROW. "Yas. I fancy it is rather grand; but then, you see, I give the whole of my mind to it."

Discernment.

CLEVER CHILD. "Oh! do look here, mamma dear, such a funny thing! Mr. BOKER's got another forehead at the back of his head."

[BOKER *is delighted.*

Life in London.

ISABELLA. "Well, Aunt, and how did you like London? I suppose you were very gay?"

AUNT (*who inclines to embonpoint*). "Oh, yes, love, gay enough! We went to the top o' the monument o' Monday — and to the top o' St. Paul's o' Tuesday — and to the top o' the Dook o' York's column o' Wednesday — but I think altogether I like the quiet o' the country."

The Husband as he ought to be, and   As he ought not to be.

ANGELINA. "Well, love, how do you think I look?—Do you like the dress?"

EDWIN. "I think it's perfectly charming!—I never saw you look better!"

ANGELINA. "Well, E.,—you don't say a word about my dress?"

EDWIN. "Eh, what? oh, ugh!—h'm—Beautiful, beautiful, beautiful!"

A Table d'Hôte at Paris.

ATTENTIVE SWELL (*to elegant and fascinating American young Lady, who has been monopolising the adjacent Gentlemen all through Dinner*). "Let me give you some of this" (*handing Article of Dessert*).

BELLE AMERICAINE. "No, thanks!—Well, then, a very little; for I guess I'm pretty crowded now!" [*Horror of Swells: triumph of neighboring Female British Contingent.*]

Another Pretty Little Americanism.

ENGLISHMAN (*to Fair New-Yorker*). "May I have the pleasure of dancing with you?"

DARLING. "I guess you may—for I calc'late that, if I sit much longer here, *I shall be taking root!*"

Yet another Americanism.

"Here, MARIA, hold my cloak while I have a fling with the stranger."

SARCASTIC PEELER. "Going to 'ave a new 'orse, then, Cabby ?"
CABBY. "New 'oss! 'ow d'ye mean ?"
SARCASTIC PEELER. "Why, you've got the framework together already !"

No Consequence.

"I say, JACK ! who's that come to grief in the ditch ?"

"Only the parson !"

"Oh, leave him there, then ! He won't be wanted until next Sunday !"

The Garret and the Conservatory.

GENTEEL PLURALIST. "What the people can want with a Crystal Palace on Sundays, I can't think! Surely they ought to be contented with their church and their home afterward."

Something like a Holiday.

PASTRYCOOK. "What have you had, sir?"

BOY. "I've had two jellies, seven of them, and eleven of them, and six of those, and four Bath buns, a sausage roll, ten almond cakes — and a bottle of ginger beer!"

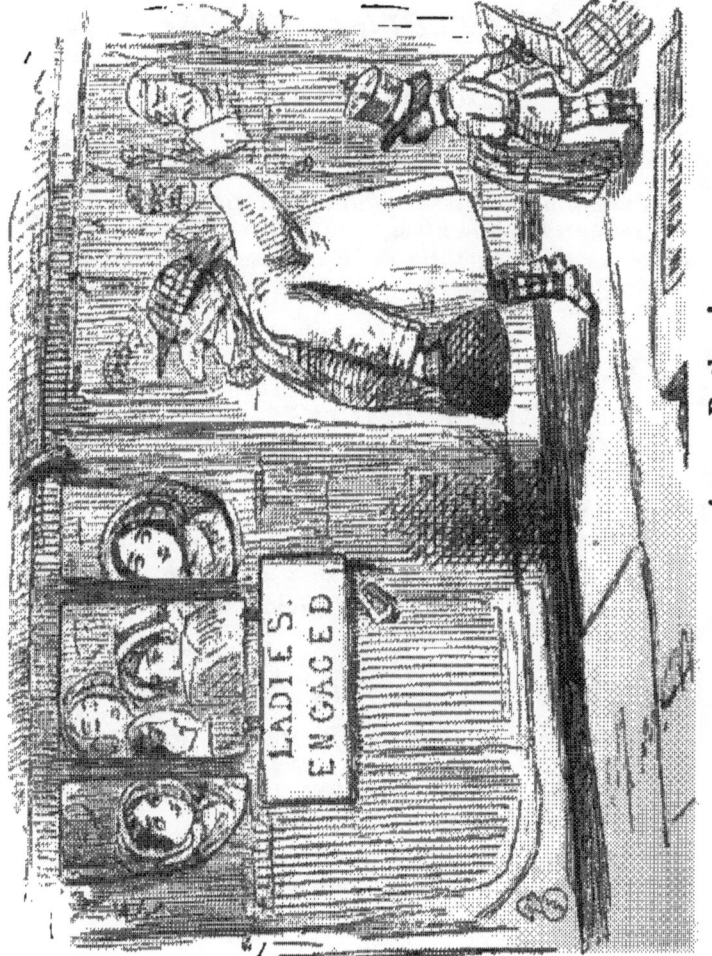

Aggravating—Rather!

The Parlor Muse:

A SELECTION OF

VERS DE SOCIETE

FROM MODERN POETS.

18mo.   Price, 30 cents;   also in cloth, 50 cents.

The selections in this little volume are of that gay and gallant order that make true *vers de société*, and represent the best writers of this kind of verse—Praed, Dobson, Locker, Aïdé, Calverley, Bunner, Gilbert, etc.   They are full of sparkle and wit, and well suited for parlor reading.

Pictures of Life and Character.

By JOHN LEECH.

FROM THE COLLECTION OF MR. PUNCH.
Uniform with Du Maurier's "Pictures of English Society."

18mo.   Price, 30 cents; also in cloth, 50 cents.

New York: D. APPLETON & CO., 1, 3, & 5 Bond Street.

NEW CHEAP SUMMER EDITION, IN PARCHMENT PAPER.

Bachelor Bluff:

His Opinions, Sentiments, and Disputations. By OLIVER B. BUNCE.

New cheap edition. 16mo, parchment paper. Price, 50 cents.

New York: D. APPLETON & CO., 1, 3, & 5 Bond Street.

The Rhymester;

or, The Rules of Rhyme.

A Guide to English Versification. With a Dictionary of Rhymes, an Examination of Classical Measures, and Comments upon Burlesque, Comic Verse, and Song-Writing. By the late TOM HOOD. Edited, with Additions, by ARTHUR PENN.

Three whole chapters have been added to the work by the American editor—one on the sonnet, one on the *rondeau* and the *ballade*, and a third on other fixed forms of verse; while he has dealt freely with the English author's text, making occasional alterations, frequent insertions, and revising the dictionary of rhymes.

"Its chapters relate to matters of which the vast majority of those who write verses are utterly ignorant, and yet which no poet, however brilliant, should neglect to learn. Though rules can never teach the art of poetry, they may serve to greatly mitigate the evils of ordinary versification. This instructive treatise contains a dictionary of rhymes, an examination of classical measures, and comments on various forms of verse-writing. We earnestly commend this little book to all those who have thoughts which can not be expressed except in poetic measures."—*New York Observer.*

"If young writers will only get the book and profit by its instructions, editors throughout the English-speaking world will unite in thanking this author for his considerate labor."—*New York Home Journal.*

18mo, cloth, extra. Uniform with "The Orthoëpist" and "The Verbalist." Price, $1.00.

New York: D. APPLETON & CO., 1, 3, & 5 Bond Street.

www.ingramcontent.com/pod-product-compliance
Lightning Source LLC
Chambersburg PA
CBHW020033030726
47499CB00007B/2402